THE LAST BIT BEAR

A Fable

D0062721

Amanda
Underwood

Taylor Trade
A Roberts Rinehart Book
A wholly owned subsidiary of The Rowman & Littlefield Publishing Group, Inc.
4501 Forbes Boulevard, Suite 200
Lanham, MD 20706

Distributed by National Book Network

Library of Congress Card Number: 2003114159
ISBN 1-57098-431-X (alk. Paper)

♾™ The paper used in this publication meets the minimum requirements of American National Standard for Information Sciences—Permanence of Paper for Printed Library Materials, ANSI/NISO Z39.48-1992.

Manufactured in the United States of America.

THE LAST BIT BEAR

A Fable

20th ANNIVERSARY EDITION

Sandra Chisholm de Yonge
drawings by **Ellen Meloy**

A Roberts Rinehart Book
TAYLOR TRADE PUBLISHING
Lanham • New York • Dallas • Boulder • Toronto • Oxford

CHAPTER I

The sun was warm and comforting. After the long, cold winter the Earth greeted the spring. In the bright sunshine, the grass turned green and young leaves clothed the bare trees.

Animals left their snug winter dens and burrows and once again moved about on the Earth. Soon nests were built and warrens were lined with fur. Everyone moved in pairs — everyone had someone, everyone but Clover. Clover was a bit-bear and he was alone. It was time for him to raise a family too, but no one — absolutely no one — was like him.

Clover searched everywhere — in dark caves, deep forests and cool swamps — but nowhere could he find another bit-bear with whom he could raise a family.

Finally he sought the wisdom of the Great White Heron — a large bird with flowing plumes and a long, yellow beak.

"Are you quite sure you have searched everywhere?" asked the Heron.

"Yes, everywhere," replied Clover. A tear fell from his eye onto his brown shaggy chest and rolled down his plump, white belly.

"Clover, come close." The Heron glanced from side to side and dropped her sharp beak to whisper into Clover's soft, round ear. "There are no bit-bears, Clover, because there is no food. The 'other animal' cut and carried away your moak trees. For weeks its presence was in the forest."

"But the tender leaves of the moak tree are my only food," cried Clover. "Where is this 'other animal'? It has always been understood that only bit-bears share moak trees."

"Shhh," hissed the Heron. "Don't say its name out loud. It appears and disappears without warning. The last thing you want to do is meet up with the 'other animal.'

"Years ago I returned to my nest and found my mate dead. While I was searching for food, he had been killed by the 'other animal.' It didn't eat him like the crocodile or vulture. It only took his beautiful plumes.

"Clover, leave this place; search other lands for your fellow bit-bears. If you remain, the end of your kind may come. Good-luck to you, Clover. Much adventure awaits you."

So, Clover put his few things in his backpack and tearfully said good-bye to his friends. There was a real chance he would never see them or his home again.

CHAPTER II

Clover traveled for many days. He left the deep forest behind. The scenery changed, but it was not pleasant. He had trouble breathing. The air was heavy with what appeared to be fog. Clover had known fog before. It was fresh and moist and left the forest as soon as the sun warmed the air in early morning. But this fog colored the sky a dull yellow; it choked Clover and made his eyes sting and his throat ache.

Clover stopped at a stream to get a refreshing drink of water. As

he bent at the water's edge a fish
popped to the surface.

"If I were you, I wouldn't drink
the water. If I had a choice, I
wouldn't live in it either," gasped
the fish.

Clover took a second look at
the water. In his haste to ease his
thirst, he had not noticed that the
stream was dark with brown foam
around the edges. He could not
even see his reflection.

"What happened? Who did
this? I have never seen such an
ugly stream!"

"It's there," the fish weakly gestured with her head, "up the hill."

Clover followed the fish's directions and to his horror saw great black clouds puffing from stacks as tall as trees. Further downstream Clover saw huge, round pipes. Steamy, black water flowed from them.

"Why?" cried Clover. "It has always been understood that the air and water are life to us."

"It's the 'other animal'," whispered the fish. "It has poisoned the air and water with its wastes. Not many animals live here anymore; they either moved away or died when the water darkened. I am the only one of my kind left, and I cannot last much longer."

"Oh!" cried Clover. "I too am alone and searching for my kind. You could travel with me; surely we could find a clear pond for you not far from here."

"Bear, how good of you. I'd love to go!"

Clover had never before seen a fish smile. But in an instant the smile was gone, and Fish's fins sagged in despair.

"But Bear I cannot live long out of water. I'll dry in the sun and die."

"Then I'll carry you. But we need something that will hold water. Hmmm." Clover looked right and left.

"I know!" cried Fish.
"Upstream there's an old,
deserted cabin. Perhaps you could
find something there."

Clover shuffled off and soon
returned with an old wooden
bucket from the cabin's well.

Clover filled it with water and
happily shouted, "Hop in!"

And Fish with a lively flip did
just that.

CHAPTER III

Clover and Fish were quite a pair.
Although Clover's feet were
always wet from water sloshing
out of the bucket, he was
delighted with Fish's company.
Fish told wonderful stories.

One afternoon as Fish rested
her fins on the edge of the bucket
and began to tell Bear an
outrageous tale, Clover saw in the
distance what appeared to be a
mountain.

As they approached the
mountain Clover and Fish found
that it was built of shiny cans,

paper boxes, old stoves and chairs, pickle jars and piles and piles of rotten food: squashed tomatoes, brown-spotted apples, black bananas and much, much more. Clover had to pinch his nose for the smell was bad, and flies buzzed about his head.

"Hee, hee, what's the matter kid, weak stomach? Welcome to my plenteous abode."

Clover looked for the owner of that sly voice and much to his surprise saw a large, fat, sleek rat. In fact, it was the largest, fattest, sleekest rat Clover had ever seen.

"What are ya doing in these parts, Bear? Not many moak trees left here anymore, just plenty of garbage," said the rat smacking his lips and running his tongue over his sharp, protruding teeth.

"He's looking for his own kind," Fish grumbled. She could not hide her loathing for the rat.

"Yeah? We haven't had moak trees in these parts for years; the 'other animal' cut them down and made this *de*licious garbage dump instead. I'd say it's quite an improvement," laughed the rat.

"You mean the 'other animal' has been good to your kind," Clover sputtered in disbelief.

"Oh, yeah," grinned the rat. "When it does good, we do good. When it chopped down the forest and poisoned the hawks and coyotes, it was good riddance as far as I was concerned. We have no enemies left — just plenty of chow.

"Course, I wouldn't say the 'other animal' and I were buddies or anything. As long as it does its thing and we stay out of its way, we win. Look around! Thanks to the 'other animal' our kind is doing just fine. Hee, hee, hee.''

As Clover and Fish glanced over the mountain of garbage, they saw rats scurrying everywhere. There must have been a thousand! Rats with their heads in pickle jars lapping up left-over juice, rats in a line feeding on a green watermelon rind, and even one rat lying on his back and flipping stale kernels of popcorn into his mouth.

''Hey, head west toward the forest. Might be a few moak trees left there. In fact, I'll take ya myself. Things are a little slow around here now. A trip'll do me good. Just a minute, I'll pack my duds."

As Rat dug through a mound of garbage and selected this and that for his suitcase, Fish did a flip in the bucket and splashed water all over Clover.

"Why'd you do that, Fish?" Clover asked as he shook himself.

"We don't need him, Clover. He will be nothing but trouble. He's fat and lazy and he'll just slow us down."

"Now, Fish, he's offered to help. Besides I can't go much farther without moak leaves and he knows where to find them. It will be fun."

By this time Rat had returned with his bulging suitcase. "Hey,

Bear, how about giving me a lift in your backpack?"

"What did I tell you?" Fish hissed at Clover.

"O.K." Clover laughed. "Hop on, Rat."

And off Clover strode with Fish fuming in the bucket and Rat clinging to his back.

CHAPTER IV

After days of travel, Clover, Fish and Rat entered the green coolness of the forest, and much to the bit-bear's delight found moak trees. "Ahhh," thought Clover, "how good it feels to sink my teeth into the fresh, crisp leaves." Yet, hungry as he was he

was careful not to damage the trees and not to take too many leaves from any tree. Satisfied, he laid in the shade of a moak tree and fell asleep.

Awooo . . . Clover was awakened by an eerie howling. The howl was long and high-pitched. It sounded like an animal in great pain. Clover rolled over and tried to sleep, but the sound was so sad he felt he had to do something. He roused himself and listened intently for the source of the wild cry. With Fish and Rat in tow, he ambled in its direction.

They did not have to wander far. As they made their way through a grove of trees, they came upon an awful scene. In a

clearing in the forest was the most
beautiful wolf Clover had ever
seen. It was gray and white and
black with a pointed snout and
sharp, alert ears. But the wolf was
a prisoner — his foot caught in

the jaws of a steel trap. The wolf
had tried to run, but the trap was
secured by a chain to a nearby
tree. He had even tried to chew
the trap from his leg, but his fine,
white teeth were no match for the
trap's steely strength.

The wolf spied Clover and cutting short a howl turned to him. "Bear," he said in a raspy voice, "if you have little fear and great strength, please help me escape this painful prison. I have been trapped for two days. I shall die without your help."

"Don't do it, Bear," Rat cautioned. "Look at those teeth. He could tear you apart in a bite. Wolves are pretty smart cookies. I'll bet it's a trap; the rest of his pack is probably surrounding us right now." And Rat, looking left and right, began backing into the forest.

Clover turned to Fish. "What do you think?"

Propped on the edge of the

bucket, Fish studied the wolf. His feverish eyes pleaded for help. His pain and fear were real.

"Bear, open the trap," Fish quietly said.

Clover gripped the sides of the jaws with his two paws, and with all his strength attempted to pull them apart. His paws were clumsy and so the task proved difficult. Finally the wolf was able to pull his foot from the trap.

"Thank you bear and you too Fish, your courage has given my life back to me. I have not seen bears of your kind in this forest for years. What brings you here?"

"I am searching for my own kind," replied Clover. "Because of the 'other animal', moak trees are becoming harder and harder to find. Bit-bears eat only the tender moak leaves and now we too are becoming scarce.''

"I know," interrupted the Wolf. "The 'other animal' cuts down the forest to build its home. Land where a wolf may live without fear is vanishing. But, enough of my troubles — let me think, how can I help you?''

The wolf thought long and hard; he tried desperately to remember when he had last seen a bit-bear. Finally with a deep sigh he had to admit that he could not help Clover.

"Thanks, anyway," said Clover. "We must be on our way; our journey seems only to lengthen with each passing day."

"Wait!" cried the wolf. "I know an animal who may be able to help you. Her wisdom and memory are vast — Numa, the great blue whale. Travel west to the Water That No Wolf May Drink. Numa passes there on the way to her summer feeding grounds. If you wait patiently on the shore by the deepest, bluest water you may be able to find her . . . and she may be just the one to help you."

So Clover thanked Wolf and with a sigh turned to leave.

"Just a moment!" shouted Wolf. "I owe you my life. I'll go with you and protect you and your friends — even Rat. There is nothing left for me. My pack has scattered. My home now belongs to the 'other animal.'"

So Clover, Fish, Rat and Wolf set out to find Numa, the great blue whale.

CHAPTER V

Weeks later, weary and foot-worn, Clover and his friends found the Water That No Wolf May Drink. As far as they could see there was water — the blue of the sky and the blue of the water melting into each other in the distance.

They waited. Day after day, they watched the sun set over the water. Finally one morning as the sky turned a brilliant orange and yellow, a large column of vapor rose out of the ocean. Clover jumped to his feet in excitement.

Yes! It was the sign of the great blue whale.

Soon the whale surfaced and Clover gasped in astonishment. Never had he seen such an animal. The skin of her long streamlined body glistened blue-black in the sunlight. Beneath her gentle, intelligent face Clover viewed the folds of skin that would open like an accordion as she scooped krill and water into her mouth.

Standing before this magnificent creature, Clover felt very small.

Clover called to the whale and she moved closer to the shore. Able to view only one side of her at a time, Clover could just see into her huge, but kindly eye.

"My friends and I have traveled a long way. Wolf told me you may be able to help me find my own kind." Clover quickly explained the moak trees and his search for a mate.

"Bear, your search will be a long and lonely one — as mine is each season," replied the whale. "Animals of our kind are few and often spread over great distances. Even if any of them are left they are very difficult to find.

"Once there were many blue whales in the sea and every spring many babies were born. But, the 'other animal' has hunted us without mercy. Now I swim the seas for months and never see another member of my family."

Expecting a magic solution to his problem and not finding one, Clover sagged with despair. "But what shall I do now?" he whispered.

"Continue to search for your own kind," replied the whale. "Keep in your heart the thought that bit-bears, whales and wolves, rats and fish and even the 'other-animal' are of one kind — the air, the water, the Earth feed us all.

One day, the 'other animal' will understand."

Clover and his friends watched the whale turn and slowly swim away.

CHAPTER VI

With shoulders sagging and head lowered in despair, Clover wandered down the beach. He followed the shoreline with no clear direction in mind.

Wolf, Fish and even Rat did their best to cheer up Clover. Wolf acted foolishly by chasing his tail; Rat, throwing sand everywhere, did somersaults after him; and Fish began her most preposterous story, ever.

Clover appreciated what his friends were trying to do. As he stopped and lifted his head to

watch their antics, he noticed in the distance a small figure. It was about his size and shape and it walked upright as he did. Was it possible? After so many miles and disappointments had he finally found another bit-bear? With great excitement Clover picked up Fish, shouted at Wolf and Rat and began running towards the small figure.

Huffing and puffing, (bit-bears almost never run), Clover approached the small creature. It was making animal shapes in the sand; Clover recognized one as the great blue whale. But to Clover's dismay, the small creature was not a bit-bear at all.

''Hello,'' said the small boy.

"What a day this has been — a great blue whale and now a bear, a wolf, a rat and a fish in a bucket! My dad will be so excited. He's a biologist. He studies animals, especially great blue whales. I'll bet he's never seen a bear like you. What's your name?

"I'm a bit-bear," replied Clover. "But why does your dad study the great blue whales?"

"To save them! There aren't many great whales left.

"But, why are you all here?"

"I'm looking for others of my own kind," replied Clover, "and my friends — they're looking for new homes."

"I may be able to help you," said the boy. "But first will you turn to the side, so that I may shape you in sand? You are the first bit-bear I have ever seen and I want to show you to my dad."

So Clover posed as the small boy shaped his head, ears, and round belly in the sand. The afternoon lengthened and Clover, Wolf, Rat and Fish played and talked and laughed with the boy. As the sun spread its final warm glow over the ocean, Clover knew

it was time to be on his way. But first he had to take care of his friends.

"You said you might be able to help my friends," said Clover. "How?"

"My Dad often takes me camping in the mountains. It's not far from here. It's a wild place and it's safe for animals. Hunters and trappers are not allowed. You know, it's called a national park."

Clover, Wolf, Fish and Rat looked at each other in confusion.

"Don't worry," said the boy, "it'll be great. There will be a fresh pond for Fish, clean air and lots of land for Wolf. But Rat . . ."

"Hey, not to worry. I'm going with Wolf and Fish. This outdoor life kind of grows on ya. Besides the junk food at the dump was ruining my teeth."

The boy said good-bye to Clover and his friends. He walked

up the beach to his father's cottage and the incoming tide slowly washed the sand bit-bear into the sea.

As Clover and his companions parted at the fork in the road, Rat shouted, "Clover, wait, our friend at the beach. I liked him, but what kind of animal was he? He never said."

As Clover sadly waved he shook his head and with a far-off look in his eyes thought of Numa, "One day the 'other animal' will understand."

EPILOGUE

In his life Clover traveled many miles, had many adventures, and made even more friends. But he never met another bit-bear. Today you will find no animal like Clover when you hike in a forest or visit the zoo. Clover was the last bit-bear.

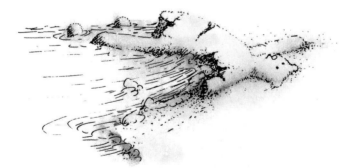